FOLLOW THE STAR

FOLLOW THE STAR

Mala Powers

Illustrations by Suzy-Jane Tanner

DAWNE-LEIGH PUBLICATIONS, Millbrae, California

THIS BOOK IS DEDICATED—

TO MY MOTHER, DELL POWERS, WHOSE DEEP INSIGHT AND DEVOTION FIRST SHOWED ME THE BEAUTY OF CHRISTMAS.

TO MY SON, TOREN. BECAUSE OF HIM, I SEARCHED FOR AND FOUND A WAY TO RECAPTURE THE INNER GLOW OF CHRISTMAS EACH YEAR.

AND

TO MY HUSBAND, M. HUGHES MILLER, WITH MY SPECIAL THANKS AND APPRECIATION. IT WAS HIS INVALUABLE GUIDANCE AND HELP WHICH HAVE MADE IT POSSIBLE FOR ME TO SHARE WITH OTHERS THE JOY OF MY CHRISTMAS EXPERIENCES IN FOLLOW THE STAR.

Dawne-Leigh Publications
231 Adrian Rd.
Millbrae, CA 94030

First Printing, September 1980

Manufactured in the United States of America

Library of Congress Cataloging in Publication Data

Powers, Mala, 1931–
    Follow the star.

    Bibliography: p.
    SUMMARY: A collection of 24 stories, tales, and legends concerning Christmas. Also includes a brief history of Advent customs and Christmas celebrations.
    1. Christmas stories.   2. Children's stories, American. (1. Christmas stories. 2. Short stories.)
I. Tanner, Suzy-Jane.   II. Title.
PZ7.P88345Fo   (Fic)   80-66664
ISBN 0-89742-046-2

1 2 3 4 5 6 7   86 85 84 83 82 81 80

TABLE OF CONTENTS

INTRODUCTION

Christmas truly captured and captivated me when I was a child and each year since, at Christmas time, I have retained much of that glow. I wanted to share with my son and my family this experience of that deeper meaning of Christmas. That's when I discovered the wonderful folk custom of daily storytelling built around an Advent calendar. On each of the twenty-four days leading up to Christmas Day itself, we would open a different window of the calendar and I would tell a story inspired by the picture we found there.

Thus began one of the richest and most joyous experiences of my life. Neighborhood children and their parents and many of our friends frequently joined in our pre-Christmas storytelling celebrations. It was wonderful to see how, through storytelling and thanksgiving, each Christmas season truly became a Christmas ADVENTure.

During the many years of my Christmas storytelling, I spent a great deal of time story searching, researching, and writing to make each evening's Christmas story and celebration ever more meaningful. Throughout these years I have had innumerable requests from families and friends to share my stories with them so they could create their own family Christmas Adventures.

Follow the Star is a collection of the best of those stories, folk tales and legends. Some have been part of Christian tradition through the centuries, and some are of modern times. The stories bear varied themes and rhythms: some are joyous, some sad; some are sweet and tender, while others tell of greed and cruelty. There is in this book a Christmas pageant of entertainment, information, truth, and legend which could not come from a single writer; nor could it come from a single period in time, but only from the hearts of people everywhere who have venerated the spirit and meaning of Christmas.

There are stories of shepherds and shepherdesses, of peasants and princes, citizens and villagers, lords and ladies, the rich and the poor and—above all— stories that tell of love, sacrifice, and service that lead to a better understanding of the true nature of Christmas.

RCA Records has recorded *Follow the Star,* blending my narrations of these stories with some of the world's best-loved Christmas and classical music. And now, here in this easy-to-read Christmas collection are those stories which have been found to have the greatest appeal to both children and adults, each given added meaning through the delightful artwork of Suzy-Jane Tanner.

These stories may be used to enrich the pre-Christmas, or Advent, season. You can heighten the adventure and anticipation of Christmas itself by reading only one story on each of the twenty-four days before Christmas. You may even use the illustrations of this book as you would the pictures of an Advent calendar.

Whether you read these stories alone or with your family, whether you read several stories at a time, or only one on each of the twenty-four days before Christmas, it is my hope that the characters and events may come alive for you as they have for so many others. I hope that Thaddy, the little blind shepherd and Chi-Wee, the young American Indian girl, and Felix and Johnny and Lolla and all the others may bring to you an insight into the excitement and love for Christmas which people have shared over the centuries. May this story-celebration of Christmas bring as much joy to you as it has to me, my family, and my friends.

MALA POWERS
North Hollywood, California

THAT CHILD WHOM CHRISTMAS CAPTURES
GROWS BEAUTIFUL AND WISE,
POSSESSOR ALL HIS DAYS OF ARTS AND RAPTURES
AND HEAVEN-DAZZLED EYES.

PHYLLIS McGINLEY

FOLLOW THE STAR

Once, high up in the heavens, there was a little gold star that could not move. It didn't shine very brightly, but the light of the star was soft and warm and gentle like the heart of the angel who lived within it.

Nearby were stars whose brilliant lights were strong and radiant. They moved in great circles and dazzling cartwheels across the heavens. But it didn't matter to the angel who lived in the little gold star that it was fixed in the heavens, for it could always gaze at the most wondrous sights. It beheld the mighty heavenly deeds of the Lord!

One day, the Father and the Son and the Holy Spirit called for a great conference in the heavens. All the heavenly host, including the star-angels, were gathered—the wondrous seraphim and the cherubim and the mighty thrones. The Archangel Michael stood tall and proud, and the angels Gabriel and Raphael had a special glow about them as if they already knew the wonderful news that God the Father was about to tell. Then God the Father spoke. "The time has come for my Son to be born as man upon the earth."

God then showed a great vision to all the heavenly host. They saw the birth of the baby Jesus. They watched Him grow into manhood and perform His miracles. They saw ahead for thousands of years as human beings chose to be aware that the Christ had been born within each one of them as well as in a stable upon the earth. And as they watched this vision, the voices of the heavenly host rang out in a great chorus of praise.

The little gold star-angel was so filled with this vision that it hardly heard God say that what was now needed was a star—a special star which men on earth could follow to the birthplace of the Christ Child.

"Which of you will shine as that special star?" asked God the Father.

"I will! I will!" cried all the heavenly host.

But for each one, God had another mission. "You, Gabriel, will appear to a maiden named Mary and tell her that unto her the Son of God is to be born as man upon the earth. And you, Raphael, will appear with the heavenly host to the shepherds on the hills of Bethlehem on the night of their savior's birth."

All were reminded of their appointed tasks until only a few star-angels remained, each hoping to be the one selected.

Now the little gold star-angel had never spoken one word, for it was still lost in the vision which God had shown.

"Why are you silent, little star-angel?" asked God the Father, although He already knew the answer. "Would you not like to lead men to my Son?"

"Oh, yes, Father God. I would like to be that star— more than anything in heaven, or on earth! But my light is so small, and I am a fixed star. I cannot move. How can I lead men to our Lord?"

"Your light is full of love, little gold star-angel. That is more important than anything!"

Then all the heavenly host agreed and together cried, "We shall help! We shall carry you on our great wings!"

"Oh, oh, thank you!" said the grateful little gold star-angel.

And so the long journey began. The little gold star was carried and helped by all the heavenly host, and its light grew brighter and more radiant as it neared the earth. The Wise Men of the East saw the star and followed it to where the Christ Child lay.

And many others followed the light of the little gold star and found the Christ when He lived upon the earth.

When that magic time was past, the outer light of the star was no longer needed by man. The angel who lived in the little gold star then went to dwell, as an inner light, with the Christ it loved and served so well—in that sacred place within each one of us.

If we choose to look into the quiet of our own hearts, we will see its light and hear its voice saying, "Follow your star, follow the star within you 'til you build a manger in your own heart where the Christ Child can be born again each year.

"Follow the star! Yes, follow *your* star!"

HEART'S DESIRE

Inside the Indian trading store, Chi-Wee saw her mother stroke a beautiful, soft wool shawl. It was dark blue on one side and glowing red on the other, with a fringe of the same two colors. Chi-Wee saw the look of longing in her mother's eyes. "My mother, you will buy this beautiful shawl?" she asked.

"No, my little one. This day the pottery I have made must be traded for food only."

"But you need a warm shawl," cried Chi-Wee. "The wind is cold! You need this shawl!"

"We will not speak of it more, my daughter," said her mother.

Chi-Wee stood looking down at the bright-colored shawl. In her heart, a fierce little voice said, "My mother shall have that shawl. The 'Good Spirit' made that shawl to be for my mother."

The shawl cost six dollars, and there were few ways for a little Indian girl of that time to earn so much money. Yet over and over again, Chi-Wee imagined putting that wonderful shawl around the shoulders of her mother.

When next they went to the trading post, Chi-Wee, with trembling fingers, thrust a pink shell necklace into the hands of the man who ran the store. It was her most precious possession!

"I know this is not enough, but could you . . . oh, could you please keep this shawl for me?" Chi-Wee pleaded. "It's for my mother. I will pay more on it the next time."

The expression in the eyes of the trader softened, and a faraway look appeared in his eyes as he said tenderly, "If she had lived, my daughter would be about your age. Yes, I will keep the shawl for you, little girl of the mesa, until you bring the rest of the money."

The following month was a very busy one for Chi-Wee. She could hardly wait for the next trading day to come, and her eyes shone with pride when she handed the trader a great jar of wild honey. Chi-Wee did not tell him of the many days of hard labor she had had in gathering it, or of the painful lumps on her arms that told of the angry stinging of the bees.

There was a look she could not understand in the eyes of the trader. "I hope you won't mind, the bright-colored shawl is gone. But I have other beautiful shawls, little girl," he said.

Chi-Wee could not speak; words would not come. Her eyes filled with tears as she ran from the store. She slumped sadly in the wagon while her mother finished her purchases. All the way home in the bumpety old wagon there was a storm of anger and grief in Chi-Wee's heart. "It cannot be true," she thought. "People cannot be so thoughtless and cruel."

When they arrived home, Chi-Wee's mother called her to help unload the parcels. "And here's one, Chi-Wee, that the trader said you had bought. With what could you buy it, my daughter?"

Chi-Wee did not wait to answer. She tore open the paper of the parcel. It was the shawl—that wonderful shawl for her mother! Tied to one corner was a note that said, "It is the love for your mother that has bought this shawl, little girl of the mesa; and it is my love for another little girl like you that gives you back your precious treasure."

Chi-Wee looked, and there, pinned to the shawl, was her pink-shelled necklace.

Tears of happiness and gratitude glistened in Chi-Wee's eyes as she wrapped the beautiful bright-colored shawl around her mother's shoulders.

Chi-Wee had learned a great secret: when we love and truly want to give, the 'Good Spirit' opens the way to our heart's desire.

A LEGEND OF THE FIRST CHRISTMAS TREE

How did the evergreen tree first become such an important part of the celebration of Christmas? No one really knows. There are many Christmas-tree legends. Could this one be true?

On a dark and wintry Christmas Eve, nearly twelve hundred years ago, Winfred the Englishman boldly walked into a large clearing deep in a forest in northern Germany. There, a blazing fire sent tongues of flames and fountains of sparks high up into the sky. Gathered in the clearing were fierce tribesmen and their families who worshiped nature and believed in human sacrifice. They watched in silence as old Hunrad, their high priest, walked slowly to the foot of a giant oak tree. Before him stood a bound and frightened young boy who was about to be sacrificed to the Norse god, Thor.

Winfred moved quietly but quickly around the silent crowd of tribesmen until he stood close to the high priest. Old Hunrad grasped a black stone sacrificial hammer. Summoning all his strength, he swung the hammer high in the air. As it poised for an instant above the boy's fair head, Winfred the Englishman rushed forward. Quickly he raised his heavy wooden staff and, before the fatal blow could fall, struck the stone hammer from the old priest's hand.

A gasp of awe sounded throughout the clearing as Winfred untied and released the frightened boy, who ran to the arms of his grateful mother.

Then Winfred, his face shining like an angel's, cried out, "Oh, tribesmen of the North and sons of the forest, no blood shall flow this night. For this is the birth-night of the Christ, the Savior of mankind. Greater is He than your old gods, Thor and Odin; more loving and more beautiful is He than your Baldur and Freya. Since the Christ has come, human sacrifice is ended. The Blood Oak tree shall stain your land no more. In the name of the Lord, I destroy it!"

Then, before the astonished eyes of the fierce tribesmen, Winfred drew forth a wooden cross and struck the giant tree. Suddenly, the Blood Oak, as if gripped by an unseen power, was ripped from its foundations. Backward it fell, groaning as it split in two and crashed to the ground.

Just behind the fallen oak, unharmed, stood a young fir tree, its branches pointing toward the heavens.

"This little evergreen shall be your holy tree tonight," Winfred told the awe-struck men and women. "It is a sign of endless life, for its leaves are always green. Gather around this tree and celebrate— not deeds of blood, but living deeds of love and rites of kindness."

Then Winfred told them of the birth of the baby Jesus in Bethlehem and of the gifts of love and mercy which Christ brought to all mankind.

And all who listened were filled with reverence and wonder, and they called the evergreen *the tree of the Christ Child* and hung gifts upon its branches. The light of the moon made the tree sparkle 'til it seemed to be tangled full of stars—and hymns of thanks were sung for the Babe of Bethlehem.

THE ADVENT WREATH

"Oh, Sally, I'm so glad you're going to celebrate Advent with us tonight!" Kathy remarked, as the two girls entered the Brandon living room where they were warmly greeted by Kathy's mother and father and four-year-old brother, John.

"I've never been to an Advent celebration before," Sally shyly told the family. "I don't even know what Advent is."

"I do!" exclaimed little John with excitement. "It's a regular Christmas adventure!"

Everyone laughed. "You're right, John!" said Mrs. Brandon, and added, "I'll explain as we celebrate Advent tonight, Sally. I think you'll understand."

A peaceful quiet soon settled through the room as Kathy's mother turned down the lights and lit some candles. "First of all, Sally," she said, "the word 'advent' means 'coming,' and for hundreds of years the Advent season, which is the period beginning four Sundays before Christmas, has been the time when people open their hearts, day by day, to the 'coming' in of the Christmas spirit of joy and peace. Then, on Christmas Eve, they are really ready to welcome the Christ Child.

"In olden days, Advent celebrations were held only in churches—often with Nativity plays, including great processions, splendid costumes and lots of glitter. But people also wanted a special, quiet *family* Advent celebration in their own homes. Of course, many different Advent, or pre-Christmas, customs arose in different countries, such as storytelling—often built around the Christmas themes pictured in an Advent calendar.

"Another ancient custom is the ringing of bells, which always seem to say, 'Pay attention! Something wonderful is coming!' "

Kathy's mother then rang a small silver bell, and her father recited a little verse called, "Bell Ringing"—

"To wonder at beauty, stand guard over truth,
Look up to the noble, resolve on the good;
This leads man truly to purpose in living,
To right in his doing, to peace in his feeling,
To light in his thinking—
And teaches him trust in the working of God,
In all that there is
In the width of the world and the depth of the
        soul."

When it was time for the Advent calendar story, Kathy eagerly picked up the brightly colored cardboard calendar. "See, Sally, it has twenty-four little windows, one to be opened for each of the twenty-four days before Christmas," she explained. "You're our guest; so you open tonight's window!"

Everyone crowded around as Sally opened the window and exclaimed, "Why, it's a picture of a green wreath with four tall candles."

"That is an Advent wreath, and *here's a real one*," said Mrs. Brandon, pointing to a small table which held a lovely, fresh evergreen wreath. "People have made them for generations, and the Advent wreath, too, has many meanings for different people. Even its four candles are symbols," she said as she lighted the first candle. "Next week, two candles will be lighted; the following week, three candles; and during the last week before Christmas, all four candles will burn side by side."

Mrs. Brandon continued, "This first candle is called the *Prophecy Candle.* It reminds us that centuries before the birth of the Christ Child, wise men called prophets foretold His birth. One prophet, named Micah, even foretold that Jesus would be born in Bethlehem!

"The second candle, called the *Bethlehem Candle,* reminds us of the little town of our Savior's birth. We picture Mary and Joseph going wearily from inn to inn, unable to find a resting place until at last they are led to the shelter of a stable. Then—on that holiest of nights—as they rested in the stable with the gentle animals, Mary's son, the baby Jesus, was born!

"The third candle is named the *Shepherds' Candle,* for it is they who came to adore the Christ Child and to spread the good news.

"The fourth candle is called the *Angels' Candle* to honor angels and the great news they brought to mankind on that wondrous night. Although we may not see or hear them, it is the angels, even to this day, who bring God's messages to us in thoughts of love and peace, joy and good will."

The Brandons and Sally then sang the lovely Christmas carol, "Away in a Manger." After they finished and Mr. Brandon said a closing prayer, everyone enjoyed a special feeling of warmth and happiness.

As Kathy and little John helped put out the candles, Mrs. Brandon remarked, "I hope you liked it and will join us again, Sally."

"Oh, yes, yes—and thank you!" Sally exclaimed happily. "It was wonderful! You know, little John *is* right! Celebrating Advent really is a Christmas Adventure."

FROM SAINT NICHOLAS TO SANTA CLAUS

The spirit of giving *has always been a part of Christmas. In every land it shows itself in a special form and in a different dress. In Spain this* spirit of giving *rides as The Three Kings, leaving gifts for sleeping children. In Italy it is La Befana, an old woman, who brings the presents. And in Sweden it is a delightful little elf, the Yul Tomten, who delivers the gifts. Yul Tomten, like all the others, tries never to let himself be seen or caught and comes only by night or in the early dawn. Luckily for us, there is also the good Saint Nicholas who, when he came to America, became Santa Claus.*

Long ago, a boy was born in a faraway country. His name was Nicholas and from early childhood he showed, in many ways, he loved God. When he grew to manhood and became a bishop, he used the great wealth that God had given him to help others. Now, Nicholas didn't want anyone to know of his loving deeds, but once he was discovered as he quietly left his gift in the middle of the night!

Nicholas had so much of the *spirit of giving* in him that his fame soon spread all over Europe. Bishop Nicholas became Saint Nicholas, and many stories and legends tell us of his wonderful deeds and generosity to all people—and especially to children. Even today, children in other countries eagerly await his coming on December 6, Saint Nicholas Day, when he brings his gifts.

The people of Holland long ago adopted Saint Nicholas as their *spirit of giving;* and, when the Dutch settled in America, they brought Saint Nicholas with them. The Dutch knew that their children would be very lonely without him.

In New Amsterdam, which later became New York, pictures of the tall, lean saint in his high hat and long red bishop's robe were seen all over the city. The Dutch children's pet name for Saint Nicholas was Sinter Klaus.

Now, when the English children who had settled in America noticed that Sinter Klaus always brought gifts to their Dutch neighbors, they asked that Sinter Klaus, or Santa Claus as they pronounced it, would visit them too! And as he loves all children, Santa Claus soon filled English stockings as well as the Dutch wooden shoes.

As the settlers became Americanized and changing times affected speech, dress, and transportation, these same changes happened to Saint Nicholas, or Sinter Klaus, our Santa Claus. His tall, pointed bishop's hat is still pointed, but it no longer stands up straight and it has a white, furry tassel on the end. Saint Nicholas' red bishop's robe has changed into a red suit, trimmed with white fur and, as our Santa Claus, he has gained a great deal of weight! Here in America he travels by reindeer sled on Christmas Eve instead of by horseback on the eve of December 6, as in Holland. And—Santa Claus has become jollier and jollier!

Yes, the *spirit of giving* shows himself in many ways and, whether he is called "Père Noël" as in France, "Weihnachtsmann" as in Germany, "Father Christmas" as in England, or "Sinter Klaus" or "Santa Claus," he excites the hearts of children everywhere. And with each toy and present that he leaves, he gives a part of himself—a gift that he hopes we will keep forever: the *spirit of giving*.

THE LITTLE BLIND SHEPHERD

Long ago, near the town of Bethlehem, there lived a young blind boy named Thaddy. He was a kind and happy child and loved to go into the hills with his father to tend their sheep. He was also a wonderfully capable boy who, even though blind, planted his own garden and sold his fresh-picked vegetables at the marketplace in Bethlehem.

One bitter winter afternoon, as he was returning home from the marketplace with his donkey, Petra, Thaddy heard the voices of a man and a woman on the road ahead. As he passed them, the woman stumbled and fell.

''Are you hurt, Mary?'' Thaddy heard the man ask anxiously.

''No, Joseph, but I fear I cannot walk even a little farther. I ache so with the cold.''

''Can I help you?'' Thaddy called out. ''My home is near here.''

''You are very kind,'' replied the lady, ''but my husband and I must reach Bethlehem before dark.''

It was so cold and the lady sounded so weary that Thaddy's heart went out to her. ''Please take my donkey. You can return him to me in a few days.''

The lady smiled and said gently, ''Why bless you, little one. But what would your parents say?''

''Oh, Petra is mine!'' said Thaddy. ''I bought him with my own money. My parents will understand when I tell them that I lent Petra to a sweet-sounding lady who needed him. Don't worry. I can find my way very well without him.''

The lady drew in a quick breath. ''Oh, Joseph,'' she exclaimed, ''this boy is blind. It is right that we should accept his kindness?''

The man's voice came quietly. ''Perhaps it is a sign, Mary.'' And turning to Thaddy, he said, ''God bless you for your kindness, my son.''

And Thaddy's heart was strangely glad as the lady rode off to Bethlehem on little Petra.

That night Thaddy went with his father to the hills to watch over their sheep. As they stood with the other shepherds, a great stillness came upon them. Suddenly the cold night air was filled with a strange sound, and the shepherds called out in fear. Then Thaddy heard the voice of an angel saying, "Fear not, for behold, I bring you tidings of great joy, which shall be to all people. For unto you is born, this day, in the city of David, a Savior, which is Christ the Lord. You shall find the babe wrapped in swaddling clothes, lying in a manger."

And suddenly, there was with the angel a multitude of the heavenly host saying, "Glory to God in the highest, and on earth peace, good will toward men." Then the vision of the angels dissolved into a bright and glittering star which the shepherds followed to a stable in Bethlehem.

As they entered the stable and crowded lovingly 'round the sleeping child, Mary's glowing eyes fell upon Thaddy.

"Why, you are the blind boy who gave us your donkey so that my journey might be easier. Reach out your arms. I will let you hold my son."

And as Thaddy held the precious bundle to his heart, his world grew bright and warm. The light became form, the form took shape, and the shape was the Christ Child lying peacefully in his arms.

For a long moment, Thaddy looked at the Christ Child in wonder, then whispered, "My lady, I can see him! With my eyes, I can see him! I do not understand, but I can see!"

When at last the shepherds took their leave, Thaddy turned to Joseph. "You will need my little donkey, Petra," he said. "Please keep him. I would like him to be *my* gift."

A CANDLE FOR MARY

It was a cold and bitter winter in Palestine. Dusk had fallen, and Anna's heart was heavy. She was no longer young, and her husband, Joachim, was even older. For many years they had prayed for a child, but their prayers had not been granted.

Now, Anna stood before an unlit candle in her darkened room. "Perhaps it is too late," she thought. "Perhaps I am now too old to bear a child. Still, our scriptures tell us that with God all things are possible! Again, as I light this candle, I shall ask God to send us a child."

As she lighted the candle, the whole room suddenly filled with a great light, and the vision of an angel appeared to Anna.

"The Lord has sent me to tell you that your prayers are granted! You will bear a daughter and you shall call her by the name, Mary. The Holy Spirit shall live within her, and her blessedness shall be greater than that of all holy women."

The bright vision of the angel then vanished! Only the flame of the candle glowed in the darkened room. Anna wept in wonder and gratitude and, as she looked at the light of the little candle, she whispered, "This candle . . . it is a candle . . . for Mary!"

What joy there was in the house of Anna and Joachim on that day when Mary was born! In praise and thanksgiving, Anna once again lighted a candle for Mary.

When Mary was still a very young child, she was taken to the temple to begin her training. There she learned about God and about the Holy Scriptures. Her lessons from the priests and from holy women were a joy to her!

As Mary grew older, her teachers and all who knew her recognized that she was full of light and that no darkness was in her. When Mary reached the age of marriage, the priests of the temple wondered how they could choose a husband worthy of Mary, this blessed maiden who radiated so much love. They resolved to let God choose. By a sign, God made it known that the husband for Mary was to be Joseph, a carpenter, and a very learned and religious man.

Soon the angel Gabriel appeared to Mary and said, "Hail Mary, the Lord is with you! Do not be afraid, for you have found favor with God. The Holy Spirit shall come to you, and you shall bring forth a son whom you shall name Jesus, and He shall be called the Son of God."

Mary wondered greatly at this, for she was still a maiden and not yet married. Yet, she bowed her head and said, "Behold, I am the handmaiden of the Lord. In everything, I shall be obedient to the will of God!"

Mary and Joseph were wed, and all about them was gladness and joy. From the depths of her heart Mary asked the Lord, "Help me to be worthy to bring up this holy Son whom You are sending to me."

Then Mary prayed and waited. She lighted candles, as her mother had before her, in praise and thanksgiving for this new life that was beginning—the life that would bring the light of the world to man!

THE ANIMALS' CHRISTMAS

Stories and legends from the earliest years of Christianity tell us of the roles played so lovingly by the animals in the Holy Birth of Jesus.

In many countries, a special Christmas "treat" is given to the barnyard animals to honor them for their presence in the stable during the birth of Jesus Christ. In Norway all hunting and fishing ceases for a time so that each one of God's creatures may know the peace and good will of Christmas.

The verses of these lovely carols tell us how each year, just at the stroke of Christmas, the barnyard beasts fall to their knees to adore the Christ Child. And how for an hour they receive the power of speech to tell again of the Holy Birth.

The gentle beasts of field and fold
On Christmas Eve, so bleak and cold,
At midnight all, with one accord,
Kneel to adore their newborn Lord.

And then to one another tell
The story that they know so well!
The tale of that first Christmas morn
When angels sang, "The Christ is born!"

Jesus, our Brother, strong and good,
Was humbly born in a stable rude,
And the friendly beasts around Him stood,
Jesus, our Brother, strong and good.

"I," said the donkey, shaggy and brown.
"I carried His mother up hill and down.
"I carried her safely to Bethlehem town;
"I," said the donkey, shaggy and brown.

"I," said the sheep with curly horn,
"I gave Him my wool for His blanket warm.
"He wore my coat on Christmas morn;
"I," said the sheep with curly horn.

"I," said the cow, all white and red,
"I gave Him my manger for his bed.
"I gave Him my hay to pillow his head;
"I," said the cow, all white and red.

"I," said the dove, from the rafters high,
"Cooed Him to sleep, my mate and I.
"We cooed Him to sleep, my mate and I;
"I," said the dove, from the rafters high.

And every beast, by some good spell,
In the stable dark was glad to tell
Of the gift he gave Immanuel,
Of the gift he gave Immanuel.

The gentle beasts of field and fold
On Christmas Eve, so bleak and cold,
At midnight all, with one accord,
Kneel to adore their newborn Lord.

CHRISTIAN IN SECRET

It had been a most difficult day for Marcus as he walked down a narrow, rain-swept street of ancient Rome. First he had been denied visiting the coliseum to watch the battles in the arena, then he had been scolded by his parents for speaking in 'an un-Christian manner.'

"Oh, by Jupiter, why did I have to be born a Christian?" he muttered. "I just don't understand it! All over Rome, Christians are hunted and tortured and crucified—and only because they try to be gentle and kind and love one another. Maybe it's not worth it. Maybe I'd rather just be a Roman and not a Christian!"

It was the year 250 A.D. by the Christian calendar. Many men, women, and children had already been martyred for their beliefs in the teachings of Jesus of Nazareth. And today Marcus had heard that stronger persecutions were to begin!

At that moment, Marcus turned a corner and entered a large square. There were crowds of people, and Roman soldiers were surrounding a group of school boys.

"The soldiers have discovered a secret meeting place of Christian youths," an old woman remarked. "They're questioning every boy they can find!"

Marcus felt a sudden wave of fear. What if the soldiers questioned him? How would he answer? If he told the truth, his father and mother and little sister could be tortured and killed. But could he lie? Could he say that he was not a Christian? He remembered the story about St. Peter, who had denied Christ three times and had regretted it all his life.

Suddenly Marcus felt his whole being cry out with startling clarity, "No, no, I *am* a Christian; I *do* love Christ; I will not deny Him!"

As Marcus cautiously turned to leave the square, a soldier saw him and shouted, "Stop that boy!"

Marcus began to run as fast as his legs would carry him. He could hear the shouts of the soldiers in hot pursuit. He raced down street after street until he reached the old paved road leading out of the city. He kept running until he felt that he could go no farther. It had become dark, and he had no idea where he was. Suddenly he came to a low stone wall, climbed over, and dropped face down on the wet earth.

"Surely I've lost them now," he thought. But still he could hear the sounds of pursuit. "Oh, Holy Savior," he prayed, "I'm so lost. I don't know what to do. Protect me and my family. Lead me."

As if in answer to his prayer, a bolt of lightning flashed across the sky. Marcus could hardly believe his eyes, for in that flash he recognized a great winged statue. He was in the Roman cemetery near a hidden entrance to the catacombs, that maze of underground tunnels and rooms where he and his family had come so many times with other Christians to worship in secret.

The shouts of the Roman soldiers were very near as Marcus left his hiding place and found the hidden entrance to the catacombs. He shivered as he groped his way down through one damp, cold passage after another.

Suddenly, in the darkness, a man's strong hands gripped him by the shoulders.

"Let me go!" Marcus cried in terror.

Almost at once, another man appeared carrying a small oil lamp and said softly, "Christ is born."

Marcus sighed in relief as he heard the familiar Christian greeting and answered, "And Christ is risen!"

Then together, they joined other men and women who were gathered in a small chamber nearby.

"All around us," a man was saying, "the Roman world is celebrating the Saturnalia—that time when the days are shortest and the outer sun shines with the least strength. But we, here in the darkness of our catacombs, celebrate the inner light, the birth of Christ on earth and in our inmost souls."

There was a great peace within Marcus as they began to chant softly, "Christ is born! Christ is born!"

"Yes," thought Marcus, "Christ is born, and tonight I know that He is born again, in me."

A GIFT FOR GRAMPS

"What are you going to give Gramps for Christmas?" Louella asked her brother as she stared at her Christmas list.

"That's just what I was going to ask you," replied Johnny. "I'm stumped." The two children were sitting alone at the kitchen table. Their half-finished Christmas lists lay before them. "Gramps always gets socks and handkerchiefs—handkerchiefs and socks," continued Johnny. "He has enough to last another hundred years!"

"I know," said Louella. "And we can't get him sports things because with his legs so full of rheumatism, poor Gramps just sits in his chair by the window. I wish we could think of something that would be fun for him every day to help him forget his pain."

So they thought and they thought. Louella closed her eyes, and Johnny stared out the window at the snowy yard. As he watched, a quick little bird flew to the window sill, looked into the room, and then flew away. Suddenly Johnny jumped up from his chair in great excitement. "I've got it!" he shouted.

"Got what?" asked Louella.

"Why, the present for Gramps. It's perfect, and the whole family could be in on it!"

On Christmas morning when Gramps had hobbled to his favorite chair by the bay window, Johnny said, "Gramps, we wanted to give you something different this year. Something that would be fun for a long time. Now turn around, and look out the window!"

Gramps turned to look. There, attached to the sill, was a wide new shelf with a molding around its edge. And on the shelf were all sorts of things that birds like to eat: seeds and suet and dabs of peanut butter and bits of dry bread.

"I made the feeding station," Johnny explained. "And Louella got the supply of bird food for you, Gramps." Johnny held his breath as he saw a snowbird perch on the edge of the feeding station and then fearlessly peck at some seeds.

"Well, I'll be . . ." Gramps said. "Look at that!"

Then, with a red and gray flash of wings, another bird swooped down.

"What in the world kind of bird is that?" asked Gramps.

"Ah," said mother, "that's where my present comes in." She reached under the boughs of the Christmas tree and pulled out a package which was hidden there. "Merry Christmas, Grandpa!"

Gramps opened the package excitedly. There before him was a big book with beautiful colored pictures of hundreds of birds. "Well, this is something!" Gramps exclaimed, turning the pages. "I never knew there were so many birds."

Sometime later, Gramps gave a shout. "A pine grosbeak! That's what that red and gray bird was: a pine grosbeak!" He grinned with pleasure at being such a good detective. He had forgotten all about his aching rheumatism!

"This is the best Christmas present I ever got," Gramps said.

Of course, Johnny and Louella received presents that Christmas, too; but what they always remembered best was the gift of giving from their hearts—a gift for Gramps.

THE HOLY NIGHT

The bible tells us little about Joseph, the wonderful man who protected and cherished Mary and the little Jesus. Legends and stories about him have come down from those times when miracles and wonders all seemed quite natural, especially on The Holy Night!

In the biting cold of that special winter night, Joseph searched everywhere for anything that would bring warmth to his wife and the little son who had just been born. Joseph went from house to house seeking help, but no one gave him the coals or kindling he needed to build a fire.

Joseph walked and walked until in an open field, at last, he saw the glow of a burning fire. He hurried toward it. A flock of sheep surrounded the fire, and an old shepherd watched over them.

As Joseph came near, three large watch dogs opened their great jaws to bark, but not a sound came forth. The dogs viciously dashed toward Joseph to bite him, but their gleaming teeth would not obey; and Joseph walked on and suffered no harm.

As Joseph approached the fire, the sheep lay so close to each other that he could not pass through them. He stepped upon their backs and lightly walked over the sheep to the fire. And not one of the animals awoke or moved.

When the shepherd, who was a surly old man, unfriendly and harsh, saw this strange man approaching, he seized a long, spiked staff and threw it at Joseph; but, before it reached him, the staff turned aside and fell harmlessly to the ground.

Joseph walked up to the shepherd and, as though nothing had happened, said kindly, "I need your help, good shepherd. Please let me have some of your live coals. My wife has just given birth to a child, and I must build a fire to warm them."

The surly shepherd would rather have refused but, seeing that Joseph had nothing in which to carry the hot coals, he laughed and said, "Take as many as you need."

Joseph stooped and picked up the live fire coals with his bare hands, laid them in his cloak, and carried them away as if they were nuts or apples. His hands were not burned, nor did the coals scorch his cloak.

The shepherd stared. "What kind of night is this," he wondered aloud, "when the dogs do not bark or bite, the sheep are not scared, the staff does not wound, nor the fire scorch?" In great curiosity, he followed Joseph until they came to a lowly stable where the shepherd saw Mary and her babe lying there on the cold straw.

The shepherd's heart was suddenly touched. For the first time, he felt a great desire to help. He took from his knapsack a soft white sheepskin and gave it to Joseph for the child to sleep on. And with that deed of kindness and mercy, the shepherd's eyes were suddenly opened and he saw what he had not been able to see before. All around him stood silver-winged angels, and the sound of their glorious praise filled the air. And, as the angels passed the Christ Child, they glanced at Him lovingly.

Then the shepherd knelt and gave thanks, for he understood how all creation was to be happy that Holy Night.

And it is still the same today. For angels are all around us, especially on the Holy Night, seeking to open our eyes and hearts to the glory of Christmas.

FELIX

A very long time ago, everyone in the little French village of Sur Varne was all bustle and stir preparing for the blessed birthday of the Christ Child. This was especially true of young Felix Michaud, the shepherd's son. It was his very own lamb, Beppo, which had been chosen to be carried as a gift to the baby Jesus in the Christmas Eve procession. This was the most important event of the year and was held in the town's great church.

Felix's greatest joy, however, was skillfully carving figures for a Christmas crèche, a miniature village of Bethlehem, with houses and people and marvelous animals! And his most wonderful carved figure was that of the baby Jesus which he carried in a pocket of his blouse. Felix longed, above all else, to study with Père Videau, the master carver of the village. But his father, a shepherd, refused to allow it.

Now, only three days before the Christmas Eve procession, Felix found that his Beppo, the chosen lamb, had disappeared. Felix hunted near and far, and it was not until he found himself deep into the forest that he realized dusk had fallen.

The forest harbored many dangerous animals, especially wild boars and wolves. So Felix wisely climbed up into a tall chestnut tree to spend the night. And just in time for soon after, a gaunt wolf passed by, sniffing and peering, but ran off just as two horsemen rode into sight.

"Oh, sirs, stop, I pray you!" cried Felix, peeking out through the branches of the tree.

The first rider, Count Bernard, quickly drew rein and, looking up in amazement, exclaimed, "Upon my word, what are you—a boy, or a goblin?"

"I am Felix Michaud, sir. I have been searching for my pet lamb, Beppo, and I live in Sur Varne."

"Sur Varne!" exclaimed the count. "You have come a long way. Well, little night owl, climb down and tonight you shall sleep in my castle. Tomorrow, we shall see about sending you home."

Felix was enchanted by the castle with its drawbridge and tall turrets. He was even more enchanted with the count's daughter, the little Lady Elinor.

Later, Felix helped rearrange the figures of the castle's Christmas crèche, and little Lady Elinor danced with delight. Then Felix timidly took the small carved figure of the Christ Child from his pocket and showed it to her.

The little Lady Elinor was so entranced with it that she called her father.

"In truth, it is a wonder!" said Count Bernard. "Who taught you the carver's craft, boy?"

"No one, sir," answered Felix. "Indeed, I wish above all things to learn from Père Videau, the master carver, but my father says I cannot. I must be a shepherd, as he is."

"Well, now," said the count, noting the sadness in Felix's voice, "we shall talk more of this later. 'Tis time for bed!"

Next morning they all said their good-byes, and when Felix reached home he was overjoyed to learn that his pet lamb, Beppo, had been found.

Christmas Eve was a lovely starlit night, and on all sides one could hear the beautiful Christmas songs that the peasants sang as they walked with lighted candles to the church. And when the great Christmas Eve procession began, there, with the shepherds, was little Beppo.

After the service, Felix felt someone pluck his sleeve and turned to see the little Lady Elinor.

"Oh, Felix," she cried. "I have such good news! My father has seen your father, and it is all settled! You will study with the Père Videau! And you will become a famous woodcarver. I know it! And, Felix, I'm sure it was your carving of the little Christ Child that did it."

Years later Felix did, in truth, become a famous woodcarver, but he never forgot that Christmas Eve of long ago. And if you ever visit a certain old French cathedral in the city of Arles, look carefully at the figure of a lamb chiseled in white stone over the great doorway. For Felix, when he carved it, would have told you that he was thinking all the while of his little pet lamb, Beppo.

CHRISTMAS CUSTOMS AROUND THE WORLD

In America, most of our Christmas traditions—evergreens, stockings hung by the fireplace, even the Christmas tree—have come to us from other countries. Just as our jolly, white-bearded Santa Claus is part of America's special tradition, so does each other land have its own special Christmas customs.

If you were in Sweden on December 13, you would see at least one young girl wearing a wreath with lighted candles on her head. For on this date, Sweden celebrates Santa Lucia Day. Every city and district, office and school chooses its own young girl to play the part of the *Lucia Bride.*

In each Swedish home, too, there is a *Lucia.* Very early in the morning, a young Elsa slips out of bed. She dresses with great care in a sparkling white dress and ties a bright red sash around her waist. Then comes the best part of all! Her mother helps to light the seven candles on Elsa's crown of evergreens.

Then Elsa, as the *Lucia Bride,* serves coffee and special Lucia cakes to the family. Every Elsa, and all of Sweden, loves this joyous festival for it reminds everyone that Christmas is drawing near.

A long way from the cold of the northern countries, Mexico, at Christmas time, celebrates the *Posadas.*

The word 'Posada' means 'inn' or 'lodging.' Each night beginning on December 16, a young Mexican boy or girl, like Carlos and Margarita, followed by a small group, sing and act out the story of Mary and Joseph seeking shelter in Bethlehem.

Carlos and Margarita tenderly take up their small clay figures of Mary and Joseph and carry them from door to door. At each door they knock, but are told, "There is no room at the inn."

Then, at last, one door opens. "You are welcome to the shelter of our stable," the little group is told. They enter into a large room where there is a scene of the Nativity, and then all say a prayer of thanksgiving.

Later there is a party; and Carlos and Margarita form a circle with other children for the breaking of the *piñata*, a colorful paper or pottery toy. When the piñata is broken, everyone scrambles for the candies and little surprise presents that fall from it to the floor!

Each night there is dancing and singing until on Christmas Eve, church bells ring out, calling everyone to midnight services.

In many countries it is on Three Kings Day, January 6, that children receive their gifts. In return, they leave offerings of straw for the horses or camels of the three Wise Men who ride through the night, bringing a gift to each sleeping child.

Then comes that time when the Christmas tree and the holly and ivy are taken down. In many French village streets, this charming carol is sung, bidding a lovely farewell to the Christmas season:

> Noël is leaving us, how sad it is to tell,
> But he will come again. Adieu, adieu
> Noël.
> The Three Kings ride away, in the snow
> and in the rain,
> But after twelve months, we shall see
> them again!

We are rich to have a heritage of so many different Christmas customs to illumine our faith and, like the *Lucia Bride*, to light the way to the happy Christmas seasons to come.

THE THIRD LAMB

High up in the mountains of the Austrian Tyrol, the men in the village of Fals have always been woodcarvers. A long time ago they carved only saints and Madonnas and figures for the Christmas crèche, for they believed that to carve anything else would be a sin.

A time came, however, when there were no more orders for the wonderful religious figures, and the wood-carvers of Fals and their children soon became poor and hungry.

One afternoon when Dritte, the master wood-carver of Fals, entered his workshop, he found a golden-haired boy playing with the wooden animals that knelt around the carved manger of the baby Jesus. Dritte, although struck by the beauty of the child, ragged and barefooted as he was, wondered why no one had told the boy that the holy animals of the Christmas crèche were not playthings.

As if reading Dritte's thoughts, the boy picked up a wooden lamb and held it to his cheek. "The Babe does not mind," the boy said softly. "He knows that I have no toys to play with."

Dritte's heart was touched. "I will carve another lamb for you, child, one that nods its head. You may come for it tomorrow," promised Dritte. "But it's strange that I have never before seen you in the village. Where do you live?"

"Out there," the boy waved his hand vaguely upward. "My father and I, together."

Next day, before noon, Dritte had finished the lamb. Soon after, a ragged gypsy girl, carrying a baby on her hip, came to the workshop begging for scraps of food. Dritte's heart was sad because there were none to give. Then the baby took hold of the newly carved lamb and, when Dritte took it from its little hand, the child cried as though its heart would break. Impulsively Dritte thrust the lamb back into the child's hand, and the baby's delighted laugh sounded throughout the workshop.

"So be it," sighed Dritte. "I will carve another lamb."

By late afternoon Dritte had just completed the second lamb when little Drino, an orphan, came to say good-bye. "Oh, what a wonderful lamb, Dritte. Can't I have it, please? Tomorrow I must leave for the orphan's home, and the lamb would keep me company."

"Yes, take it with you, Drino," said Dritte gently. "I'll carve yet another lamb." And he did! But the golden-haired boy did not return, and the third lamb stood unclaimed on the workshop shelf.

As times grew even worse in the village, Dritte, for the first time, began to carve animals and toys for the village children to take their minds from their hunger. Then one day a visiting merchant offered to buy all the toys Dritte could produce. But Dritte refused to carve toys for profit.

"I'll be at the village inn, should you change your mind," said the merchant.

"I cannot change my mind, sir," said Dritte, "unless God should give me a sign."

Soon after, the village priest stopped at the workshop to ask Dritte for the third lamb, which still stood upon his shelf. It was for little Marte, who was very ill. "Yes, of course," said Dritte. "I shall take it to her."

As Dritte returned from Marte's house and crossed a snowy field, the golden-haired boy suddenly appeared before him. "Dear child," Dritte cried, "I kept the third lamb until today, but you never came. I will gladly make you another."

But the boy shook his head. "I do not need another," he said. "The lambs you gave to the gypsy child and to Drino and Marte, you gave also to me."

Then the boy stretched out his arms, and in the soft mysterious light around him Dritte saw the shadow of the cross upon the snow. At last he understood and dropped to his knees.

"Don't you see, Dritte?" said the boy, smiling. "To make a toy may serve God's glory just as well as to carve a saint. The laughter of one happy child is as sweet in God's ears as the praises of angels."

A moment later, the boy had gone.

That night Dritte called upon the merchant at the inn. "I will make the toys you want," he said.

"So," murmured the merchant, "you did change your mind."

"No," answered Dritte with shining eyes, "but I have had my sign from God!"

THE CHRISTMAS ROSE

Legends and stories from earliest times, told and retold, tell us that long, long ago the stars sent messages to men on earth; but, as time passed, the stars became silent, for men no longer understood their language. The three Wise Men who traveled to Bethlehem to worship the newborn Christ Child still understood the language of the stars. A few privileged others also heard a little of what the stars had to say.

One of these was a humble shepherdess named Joanna. How she loved to watch the movements of the stars through the long nights as she sat tending her sheep on a hillside near Bethlehem! She listened to the messages of the stars, and she learned many things. Sometimes she heard their names—not the names known to the learned men, but their real, true names: the heavenly names that the star-angels call each other.

Now, for some time Joanna had observed something new and strange happening in the winter sky. From far, far away, a warm and radiant light had begun to shine. It was the light of a star which grew brighter as each night it moved closer and closer to earth, until it seemed to fill the entire sky as it hovered over the town of Bethlehem. Joanna yearned to know what was happening and asked the star to tell her. The star did not answer. As her yearning grew, she begged the star to tell her; but still the star was silent. Then one night, as she sat watching, she opened her heart in love and wonder and prayed with all her might:

> Star of wonder, star of light,
> Radiant star that shines so bright,
> I pray you may, I pray you might
> Speak to me, this wondrous night.

Suddenly a ray of light came down to Joanna with a shimmering message from the angel who lived within the star. "The Son of God is born upon the earth, little Joanna. I have come to light a pathway for those who, like you, have an open heart to understand what they see and hear. Follow me, and I will lead you to the Holy Child."

Joanna, her face aglow, arose to follow the star. Then tears came into her eyes. "I have nothing to bring with me," she cried. "The Son of God must have a gift of greeting!"

"Do not weep, gentle shepherdess. Take as your gift these greetings from all the stars." At once, with the message, rays of starlight streamed down from the heavens and, where they touched the cold winter earth, star-shaped blossoms sprang forth.

Joyfully, Joanna gathered the blossoms and followed the star rays as they led her on into the town of Bethlehem and to a humble stable.

Mary was holding the Holy Child in her arms as the gentle shepherdess entered. "We have been waiting for you, Joanna," Mary said. "Come, bring your precious flowers so that my Son may remember the gift and joy of the star world while He is here on earth."

And as Joanna knelt in rapture and offered the blossoms to the baby Jesus, He looked at her with a radiant smile and reached out. As His tiny fingers touched the blossoms, golden centers formed within the flowers, and the Christmas Rose came into being. And it blooms each year, in the cold of winter, to remind us of the star-gift, brought by the little shepherdess, nearly 2,000 years ago.

A CHRISTMAS GIFT FOR THE GENERAL

It was the year 1776; and the day was December 25. "What an awful Christmas!" thought Kennet. "It's bad enough having King George's Hessian soldiers quartered here in Trenton—but now everyone says that General Washington is going to lose the war because our soldiers are so cold and hungry!"

Careful not to awaken his grandfather, who was dozing by the fire, Kennet opened the kitchen door and slipped outside. With his faithful dog, Toby, at his side, he ran along the New Jersey shore of the ice-choked Delaware River until he reached an old boat shed. The shed held Kennet's treasure, a roomy iron-keeled boat, named the *Madcap.*

Kennet waited inside the boat shed until he heard the low whistle—a special signal. Then he cautiously unlocked the door and in came a ragged, but proud-looking stranger whom he had met in the woods only the day before.

"So, you did come!" the man said gratefully.

"Of course," Kennet replied, "and I've brought food for you as I promised."

"You didn't mention to anyone that you saw me?" the man asked anxiously.

"Oh, no, not even to my grandfather."

"Good! So much depends on it!"

Unable to resist any longer, Kennet boldly asked, "Are you a soldier? My father is a soldier with General Washington. And I'd like to believe that today, on Christmas Day, someone is helping him! I wish that . . ." Kennet stopped, for his dog, Toby, had begun to bristle and growl.

There suddenly came a sharp pounding on the door, and a voice commanded, "Open! Open, in the King's name!"

Quickly the stranger leaped into Kennet's boat and pulled the canvas cover over him. Kennet unlocked the door, and a Hessian soldier burst in.

"What are you doing here, boy?" the soldier demanded. "Who is with you?"

"N-n-no one," stammered Kennet.

"You're lying! I heard someone's voice." The Hessian took hold of Kennet and shook him fiercely.

With a growl, Toby rushed at the enemy and sank his teeth into the soldier's leg. At that moment, the ragged stranger leaped from his hiding place and, with one blow, knocked the Hessian unconscious.

As the stranger bound and gagged the soldier, he said, "It will take some time for the Hessian to get loose. You must go home at once, and I must continue on . . . Wait a minute—whose boat is this?"

"The *Madcap?*" Kennet hesitated. "Why—why she's mine."

"Then sell her to me!" the man said, urgently. "I can't explain, but I've got to have this boat."

Kennet's heart sank. Sell the *Madcap!* How could he? He loved that boat! Yet as he looked hard at the gallant, determined stranger, he swallowed the lump in his throat and said, "You may take my boat. I cannot sell it! I give her to you as a Christmas gift."

Together they launched the boat, and the stranger jumped aboard. "I'll tell you this, Kennet," he said. "Your Christmas gift is not for me. It is for a great man who guides your fate, and mine, and all America's. This gift will be delivered to him!"

On December 26, 1776, The Hessian troops in Trenton, New Jersey, surrendered to General George Washington and his men.

On the morning following, Grandfather told Kennet, "It's incredible. They say he crossed the Delaware in small boats. They say that one of General Washington's officers had been here for several days, getting the boats by one means or another."

Kennet's heart raced. His *Madcap,* he knew, was one of those boats. What if General Washington himself had been riding to victory in Kennet's very own boat!

"Yep, the tide has turned," said Grandfather, "and now we will win!"

"How lucky I am," thought Kennet gratefully. "I've been able to give a Christmas gift for the General—for America—and for freedom!"

PICCOLA

Little Piccola's heart was always warm and cheerful. Lovingly she sang as she helped her mother in their stone cottage.

She scoured the pots and pans, and she tended the geraniums that bloomed in the windows. She dragged in great armfuls of wood for the fire, made the fire, and scrubbed the floors.

"My Piccola is busy as the bee," said her mother.

"My Piccola is joyous as the lark," said her father.

Piccola brought laughter to the family, even through the many long winter evenings when none of them had had quite enough to eat.

Hard times had come to the family in their small French village by the seacoast. Piccola's father, a fisherman, had been very ill and could not go to sea, and her mother struggled to feed her family through that long, hard winter. In spite of all the hardships, Piccola's faith remained always strong.

"Spring will soon come for us," she would say, "and summer, too; and then, dear Papa, you will be well and strong again."

As the weeks slipped by and the family's little store of money grew smaller and smaller, Piccola's laughter still rang throughout their cottage; and when the holidays came, she cried out, "Oh, how I do love Christmas!"

"Dearest Piccola," said her father sadly, "you must know that this year we are so poor that we cannot have even a single gift for you."

Piccola heard what he said, but did not doubt at all that something beautiful must befall each and every child upon the Christmas Day.

On the night before Christmas, after Piccola had finished her work, she seized her father and mother by the hands.

"Let us go out and share in the Christmas joy!" she pleaded.

So they left their own small, dark cottage and went out into the village. Throughout the village and in each cottage, all the windows were decorated for Christmas and ablaze with candlelight. So close to the street were the little stone houses that, in each one, Piccola and her mother and father could see and hear the happiness and Christmas cheer within.

"Every house but ours is joyous," sighed the father.

But Piccola did not even hear him. She was laughing, and her eyes sparkled with joy. "How rich we are," she said, "for all the ornaments and cheer in each door and window are ours to enjoy!"

When at last they returned to their little cottage, Piccola kissed her parents goodnight and said, "Now I shall set out my shoe for my Christmas gift."

"Oh, Piccola," cried her mother, almost in tears, "there can be no gift for you this year." Even so, Piccola's small wooden shoe was set by the fireplace, and they all went off to bed.

Full of faith as always, Piccola awoke with the gray dawn and crept quietly to the fireplace to look into her shoe for her Christmas gift.

"Father! Mother! Come quickly!" she cried. "Look! See what the good Saint Nicholas has brought!" And there in Piccola's little wooden shoe was a tiny shivering baby bird.

"It probably fell out of its nest and down the chimney into her shoe," remarked her father.

Piccola paid no heed. The baby bird had come as her Christmas gift! She knew! And her joy was so full, as she cuddled and warmed

and fed the tiny bird, that soon her father and mother caught her joyful spirit, and they were warmed and became happy too.

So, Christmas came to Piccola, rich and full, because the spirit of Christmas was always in her heart!

Children, this story I tell to you
Of Piccola sweet and her bird is true;
In the far-off land of France they say
Her spirit lives to this very day.

HOW SANTA CLAUS FOUND THE POORHOUSE

Heliogabalus, or "Gobaly," as everyone called him, was shoveling snow as Methuselah limped up the path to watch him. Little lame Methuselah (who everyone said had been born "looking old") and Gobaly were two of the town's poor. They had lived, all their young lives, at the poorhouse.

"Ya know tomorrow's Christmas?" Gobaly asked.

"Oh, is it?" replied Methuselah. "I sure hope Mrs. Pynchum doesn't find out! She gets most disagreeable on holidays!"

The 'disagreeable' Mrs. Pynchum was in charge of the poorhouse, and everyone feared her. Methuselah continued, "Gobaly, do you believe there really is a Santa Claus?"

" 'A course there is," declared Gobaly. "I know 'cause I've seen the presents he's brought to boys and girls in the village."

"Then why don't he ever come here to the poorhouse and bring some?" asked Methuselah.

"Well," replied Gobaly, "we're on a pretty crooked road, ya know. Maybe Santa Claus just can't find the way." Gobaly always tried to show the bright side of things to Methuselah, even when there wasn't any!

Just then a runaway horse galloped across the road and ran down a poor dog, which fell helpless and howling into the snow.

Gobaly ran to help the dog and found that its leg was either badly sprained or broken. He made a splint and bound up the dog's leg.

Gobaly then discovered, from the dog's collar, that it belonged to a Dr. Carruthers, a famous physician who often visited the village. Gobaly carried the little dog to the doctor's house.

Dr. Carruthers was a big, jolly-looking man with white hair and a long white beard, who looked just like a picture of Santa Claus. The doctor petted and fussed over the dog. Turning to Gobaly, he asked who had set and splinted the dog's leg.

"Why, I did, sir," Gobaly answered, and then he told the doctor about all the other sick animals he had nursed back to health.

Dr. Carruthers looked at him intently and said, "You are a remarkable boy!"

After asking Gobaly more questions about himself, Dr. Carruthers said, "You know, I need a young helper and I think you are just the boy for the job. How would you like to come to live at my house and learn to become a doctor?"

Gobaly was almost speechless. To get away from the terrible Mrs. Pynchum and not be "town's poor" anymore; to learn to be a doctor! "Oh, oh ye-ss, yes, sir! Oh. . . ."

Suddenly the brightness faded from Gobaly's eyes. If Gobaly went away, who would take care of little lame Methuselah?

"I . . . I thank you sir," he said, "but I can't go, sir!" And before the doctor could see his tears, Gobaly turned and ran out of the house.

That night, on Christmas Eve, to everyone's joy Mrs. Pynchum went to a festival in the village. Suddenly there was a knock at the door, and who should be standing there but the good Doctor Carruthers, loaded with presents.

When Methuselah saw the doctor, with his long white beard, he gasped, "It's Santa Claus! Oh, my, I'm so glad you've come, Santa Claus. You look just like your pictures!"

The doctor laughed and, as he handed a brightly colored package to the little boy, he noticed Methuselah's lameness and he inquired about it. After a moment, Dr. Carruthers said, "I know of a hospital in the city where you might be cured. Do you have any relatives or friends?"

"Oh, yes," Methuselah answered quickly, "I've got Gobaly!"

The doctor looked sharply at Gobaly. "Is he the reason you wouldn't go with me, my boy?"

"Well I'm . . . I'm all he's got," said Gobaly.

The doctor was deeply moved. Then he said, "Suppose I take Methuselah to live with us, too?"

This time, Gobaly didn't mind if anyone saw his tears, and Methuselah clapped his hands for joy. Of course he didn't know then what was in store for him: that he would soon be cured, and that Gobaly would one day become a famous surgeon. All that Methuselah now understood was that Santa Claus was taking him away with Gobaly. Now wouldn't you agree that Santa Claus had found the poorhouse?

GIFT FROM THE EARTH

It was the night before Christmas near a small Costa Rican village. Everything was very still in the little hut made of straw and shaped like a beehive. The bright-colored parrot now dozed quietly on his perch, and three black-eyed little girls—Claudia, Márgara, and Teresa—were fast asleep on their mattress made of large dry leaves.

Antonia and José, the parents of the three girls, squatted on the earthen floor building a manger, as they did every Christmas Eve. But this year, they were both very sad for they knew their little girls—their chiquitas—had been praying that the Christ Child would bring them a doll on Christmas Day. And José and Antonia knew that their small savings would have to be used only for seeds to replant their field.

Early on Christmas morning, even before the chiquitas were awake, José was at work digging into the rich black earth to plant the seeds for his next crop. Suddenly his shovel struck something hard which he thought was a rock! Then he began to tremble with excitement, for he saw that the "rock" was really a red clay doll. Yes, here was a real doll buried in the earth! José lifted it carefully and ran to the hut.

"It's heaven's gift from the earth!" his wife, Antonia, said. They hurriedly placed the doll at the foot of the manger so that, when the chiquitas awakened, they would find her as their Christmas gift.

"The Christ Child has come!" the little girls shouted when they found the doll. "Papa, Mama, look! The Christ Child has not forgotten us!"

How excited everyone was. Even the rooster strutted in with his eight hens, and their big brown pig sniffed and grunted curiously around the doll until José chased the animals away.

Many happy weeks passed for the three girls as they took turns in dressing and undressing their doll in the clothing their mother made from old flour sacks.

Then one evening an elegant stranger, riding on a fine chestnut horse, stopped at the straw hut to ask for a drink of water. As he drank, the stranger's glance fell on the doll. The chiquitas' round eyes followed him as he carefully picked up the doll and examined her. Then he scratched her with the nail of his thumb, and some of the red clay fell away.

"Where did you get this figure?" the stranger asked. And, when he had heard the story, the man said, "Well, you certainly had a lucky Christmas!" Then the stranger pointed to where he had scratched the doll. "See," he said, "under the coat of red clay she is made of solid gold! Dolls like these were made by the Mayan Indians. In my country, the United States, they are very valuable. Will you sell her to me?"

Antonia and José looked delighted, but the stranger noticed tears in the eyes of the three chiquitas. "Don't worry, little ones!" he said. Then the stranger promised to send three dolls from America, one for each of the chiquitas. He paid José a great deal of money for the Mayan Indian doll and rode away.

As weeks passed, the chiquitas began to fear that the American had forgotten them. Then one day their father returned from the village, carrying three long boxes; and in each box was a wonderful doll.

"Qué linda! How beautiful!" said Claudia.

"Sí, qué linda!" said Márgara.

"Qué linda! How beautiful!" said Teresa, holding her doll close in her arms.

"Yes, beautiful! You are all beautiful," said their father, his eyes shining as he saw the joy of his daughters. "Ah, chiquitas, how good . . . how good was our Christmas gift from the earth!"

LEGENDS OF THE BIRDS

Before blessed Mary had breathed His name,
  Jesu,
The birds of the air, all swiftly they came
  to Jesu;
Like feathered thoughts from high above,
They sent their songs and gifts of love,
  to Jesu, Jesu, Jesu.

From out of a wood did a cuckoo fly,
  Cuckoo,
He came to a manger with joyful cry,
  Cuckoo;
He hopped, he curtsied, round he flew,
And loud his jubilation grew,
  Cuckoo, Cuckoo, Cuckoo.

A pigeon flew over to Galilee,
  Vrercroo,
He strutted and cooed, and was full of glee,
  Vrercroo,
  And showed with jeweled wings unfurled,
   His joy that Christ was in the world,
    Vrercroo, Vrercroo, Vrercroo.

    A dove settled down upon Nazareth,
     Tsucroo,
     And tenderly chanted with all his
     breath
      Tsucroo:
       ''O You,'' he cooed, ''so good
        and true,
         My beauty do I give to You—
         Tsucroo, Tsucroo, Tsucroo.''

Before blessed Mary had breathed His name
   Jesu,
The birds of the air, all swiftly they came
   to Jesu
Like feathered thoughts from high above,
They sent their songs and gifts of love
   to Jesu, Jesu, Jesu.

Through all the ages, since the star first lighted the sky over Bethlehem and the birth of the Christ Child, legends, poems, carols, and stories have reminded us of the devotion of birds to the Holy Family.

    The gleaming black raven, it is told, was the first to hear of the birth of our little Lord. As he flew at night over the gentle hills near Bethlehem, angels suddenly appeared and told him the wondrous news! At once he took the joyous message to all the birds.

    The stork, as soon as she heard the news, flew to the stable and plucked the feathers from her own breast to make a soft and downy pillow for the Holy Child. Then came the tiny wren who carefully wove a blanket of tender leaves and grass to cover Him, and the nightingale sang a lullaby, all the night long to soothe the babe into sleep. As dawn approached and the air grew chill, another gift, a loving sacrifice, was needed; and so appeared another generous winged friend.

THE ROBIN

In the stable where the Holy Family was sleeping, the fire was dying. Soon there were only a few smoldering embers, and the weary husband and wife grew cold and stirred uneasily in their sleep.

Because the Heavenly Father would allow no harm to come to them, or to the sleeping child, a little brown bird flew into the stable and swooped down to a log near the coals. He began to flap his wings, fanning the embers until they glowed. The robin's small brown breast reddened with the heat that came from the fire, but he would not leave his task. Hot sparks began to fly from the coals and burned at the feathers on his breast; but still he would not leave his task, until at last all of the coals burst into flame. The robin's tiny heart swelled with pride and happiness as the baby Jesus felt the warmth and smiled.

And the breast of the robin has remained red ever since, as a sign of his devotion to the Babe of Bethlehem.

WHY THE CHIMES RANG

There was once, in a great city, a truly wonderful church. Anyone standing at the front doorway could scarcely see to the other end where the marble altar stood. At one corner of the church a great stone tower rose so high into the sky that only in very fair weather could anyone see to the top. Far up in this tower were chimes which everyone said were the most beautiful sounding bells in the world, but no one still living had ever heard them!

They were very special Christmas chimes; and it was only on Christmas Eve that they could sound and be heard, and then, only when the greatest and best offering to the Christ Child was laid on the altar. Alas, for many long years no offering had been made that was great or good enough to deserve the magic sound of the chimes.

Still, every Christmas Eve, people crowded to the altar carrying their gifts—all trying to outdo the others without giving up anything they really wanted for themselves. Although the church was crowded and the service splendid, only the roar of the wind could be heard far up in the stone tower.

Now, in a country village some distance from the city lived a boy named Pedro, and his little brother. They had heard of the famous Christmas Eve offerings, and all year long they made plans to go to the beautiful service and worship the Christ Child.

Early on the day before Christmas, with snowflakes falling, Pedro and his little brother began their long journey. By nightfall they had almost reached the gate of the city when, there on the ground before them, they saw a poor woman who had fallen in the snow, too sick and tired to reach a shelter. Pedro knelt down and tried to rouse her, but could not.

"It's no use, Little Brother," said Pedro, "she is too heavy for us to carry. You must go on alone."

"Me? Alone?" cried Little Brother. "But then you won't be able to see the Christmas festival."

"That can't be helped," said Pedro. "Look at this poor woman. Her face looks like the Madonna in the chapel window. She'll freeze if we both leave her. Everyone has gone to the church now, but I'll stay here and care for her until the service is over. Then you can bring someone to help. Oh, and here, Little Brother, take this small silver coin and lay it down on the altar as my offering for the Christ Child. Now run, hurry!"

And as Little Brother left for the church, Pedro blinked hard to keep back his tears of disappointment.

At the great church, the service that Christmas Eve was more wonderful than ever! The organ played and the people sang, and at the close of the service poor men and rich men marched proudly to the altar to offer their gifts. At the last, the king of the country walked up the aisle and set down the royal crown as his offering!

A great sense of excitement filled the church. "Surely," everyone murmured, "we shall hear the chimes now!" But only the cold, old wind was heard in the tower.

The people shook their heads in disbelief and doubted if the chimes had ever really been heard at all.

The procession was over, and the choir had begun the closing hymn when suddenly the organist stopped playing as though he had been struck; for all at once there came the beautiful sound of chimes, rising and falling, from far up in the tower. The people in the church sat, thrilled and silent. Then, as one person, they all stood up and stared toward the altar to see what great gift had finally awakened the long-silent bells.

But all that any of them saw was the childish figure of Little Brother, who had crept silently down the aisle to lay Pedro's silver coin on the altar.

ADVENTURE TO BETHLEHEM

The sun was high in the sky as Kor slowly returned to consciousness. Although barely awake he heard a man's voice saying, "The black boy is still weak and cannot walk. Carry him to my tent."

Later in the caravan tent, when Kor was strong enough to talk, he told his story to Nathanael, the wealthy and warm-hearted Hebrew merchant who had rescued him.

"My name is Kor. I have traveled all the way from Africa with my master and teacher, Rab Casper," the boy explained. "As we were crossing this desert wilderness, a blinding storm of sand came. I became separated from my master and lost my way. Then I stumbled. I remember falling down a steep hill—then nothing more, until now."

"Praise be to God that we found you in this wilderness," said Nathanael gently. "Is your master a black man, too?"

"Oh, yes, sir. Where we live, all the people are black. My master is wise in the star wisdom of the Magi. He says that a great star has appeared which tells of the birth of God's own Son on earth! We were on our way to Jerusalem to meet other wise men and to search for the Infant."

The Hebrew merchant looked at the boy intently. Was it possible that the long-awaited Messiah was truly about to be born? After a moment, Nathanael spoke.

"I wonder . . . one of our prophets has told that a Messiah will someday be born in Bethlehem in Judea."

"Then I will go to Bethlehem!" exclaimed Kor.

Nathanael nodded in understanding; and, when the time came for them to part, he gave Kor a rough map and one of his own camels for the journey.

Nathanael embraced the boy, and said, "May you find your master and—the Child. God be with you, my young friend."

Kor traveled day and night until at last he neared Bethlehem. As he stopped at a roadside well to drink and rest, suddenly and without warning a gang of rough-looking men appeared and seized the camel. They tried to capture Kor to make him a slave, but the young black boy was too quick. He twisted and dodged and ran away so swiftly that he soon left his pursuers far behind. Although breathless, Kor kept on running. "I must get to Bethlehem," he panted, "I must!"

Suddenly, Kor stumbled over a rock and fell onto the rough road. When he tried to rise, he felt a sharp pain in his ankle and found that he could not walk! Panic gripped him. He was alone and defenseless in a strange land. What could he do? To whom could he turn for help?

Then he remembered what his master had often told him. "Fear only brings more fear. When you let fear live in your house, it brings all its relatives: panic, terror, and confusion. Drive out fear! Be master of your own house!"

"I am master here!" Kor said aloud, and at once he grew quite calm. He searched for and found a fallen branch and, using it as a crutch, he hobbled on toward Bethlehem.

Later, as Kor reached the entrance to the little town, he saw an old lame beggar sitting by the gateway.

"I am looking for a baby newly born here in Bethlehem. Can you help me?" he asked the old man.

"Well, there may be many, but I know of only one," said the old beggar. "A baby boy, born to a couple from Nazareth. They're staying quite near here," he continued, pointing the way. As Kor departed he called out warmly, "I hope he's the baby you're looking for."

When Kor reached the top of the road, his heart was beating wildly. Would this be the child? It was still daylight. There was no star to guide him. How would he know?

Kor drew near to a woman who sat under a tree, gently rocking a baby. As he heard the sound of her voice, singing a lullaby, all his pain and tiredness vanished. Kor knew his long search was over. Tears rushed into his eyes, and a small sob of ecstasy escaped his lips. The woman looked up and a faint astonishment appeared in her eyes as she saw the young black boy approach, ragged and bruised. Then Mary smiled and held out the little Babe for him to see.

Kor sank to his knees in veneration. Then Mary said with gentle wonder, "Why, you have recognized my Son. How did you know?"

"I have come a long, long way, searching for Him. But oh, Holy Mother, forgive me; I have brought no gift for Him!"

"Oh, beautiful boy!" said Mary, with a radiant smile. "Do you not know that your struggle to find Him is the greatest gift of all!"

That night, Kor was awakened by voices. There by the light of the brilliant star above, he saw his beloved master with two other Wise Men. Humbly and joyfully he watched as they reverently came with gifts to adore the Child for whom all the wise men of the ages had waited.

DON PEDRO'S CHRISTMAS

Madre Marta was firm in declaring that Don Pedro could not go to the Christmas Eve service with Lolla.

"But Don Pedro is so good," begged Lolla. "He works all the time. I would just tie him up outside the church door. I know he would be quiet."

"All right," sighed Lolla's mother, finally agreeing, "take him along if you wish." Lolla's face was radiant as she ran out from the small, square adobe dwelling in the New Mexican valley where they lived, and hurried to her pet.

"My good little burro," she exclaimed, throwing her arms around the donkey's shaggy neck, "I just couldn't go to church without you." Lolla was lucky that she could express her love to Don Pedro in words, while he could only twitch his ears to show his affection.

The weather had been very warm and, on this particular day before Christmas, it was unusually hot. "If the heat spell goes on," Lolla's father said, "too much snow will melt in the hills and the river could overflow!"

As darkness came, the family prepared to go to the church; and Lolla went to get Don Pedro, but the little donkey was not in his shed.

"Don Pedro has wandered off," Lolla called to her mother. "I will find him and meet you at the church."

She took a lantern and began her search. It wasn't far from the adobe house to the church—just down the road, over the river's bridge, and up to the small steepled chapel. As Lolla searched for Don Pedro, she saw the people of the valley walking or driving their cars to the midnight service.

After looking everywhere for Don Pedro, without success, Lolla started walking toward the church. As she crossed the old bridge she felt it sway more than usual. The water in the river was very high. How black it was, how swift!

Suddenly, Lolla's heart began to pound. Something was moving near the river's edge.

"Who's there?" she called out. In response came the loud, raucous braying of a donkey.

"Don Pedro!" Lolla gasped and, sliding down the bank to the water's edge, she found her little burro! There he was, stuck in the mud and water by the bridge. Lolla set down her lantern and, quickly wading out into the rising river, she stretched out her arms and seized her pet's tail in both hands. "Kick, Don Pedro," she commanded, "kick as hard as you can!"

Don Pedro obeyed as Lolla tugged with all her might, and at last the little burro kicked himself free of the mud and came charging out of the water.

As Lolla picked up the lantern, its light disclosed something that made her gasp. "Don Pedro," she cried, flinging herself upon the little donkey's back, "go quickly. Go as fast as you can!"

Inside the old church good Padre Carlos had just finished telling of the joys and blessings of Christmas. Suddenly the door of the church swung wide, and up the aisle came, of all things, a little burro, soggy and wet and covered with mud.

"What sacrilege is this?" cried the padre. "Such a disturbance in a church!" Then he saw the small girl, almost as wet and muddy as the donkey.

"Oh, Padre," Lolla cried, "I'm so glad we got here in time. The bridge is all washed out at the bottom. If anybody drives over it in a

car, it will fall. People will be killed." The congregation rose to its feet in alarm as Lolla blurted out her story.

When she finished, Padre Carlos touched the little donkey with tender hands. "God works in mysterious ways," he said. "Let us give thanks that perhaps lives have been saved through Lolla and this little burro."

Lolla glanced at Don Pedro quietly standing beside her. As she lovingly scratched the fuzzy head, she remembered another little donkey who had stood by the baby Jesus in a stable nearly 2,000 years earlier.

"Yes," she thought, "Don Pedro has a right to be here in church on this Christmas Eve."

THE NATIVITY

Come and join with me on a special Christmas journey. Your space and time ship is your own God-gift of imagination. Let us, together, follow the star back in time for nearly 2,000 years. Imagine yourself, perhaps hand in hand with someone you love, standing at the gate of Jerusalem. The crowd of people does not notice us, for we are dressed just as they are.

Suddenly we catch our breath, for there approaching on tall camels are three kingly looking men: one is dressed in magnificent red; the second wears a garment of shining blue; costly green robes gleam against the dark skin of the third man. It is not only their rich garments that make us stare; it is the expression on their faces. They have a radiant look, an eager look—as though at any moment they expect to experience something wonderful.

The camels stop, and one of the three men addresses the crowd. "Good citizens of Jerusalem, can you tell us where is He that is born King of the Jews? We have seen His star rise in the east and have come to worship Him."

The people begin to whisper all around. "King of the Jews? What does he mean?" the people ask. "We don't know anything about a new King of the Jews. Yet these are Wise Men—Magi—who study the stars. They must know some secret. What can be happening? What is going on?"

"Herod is king here and has been for many years," answers a man in the crowd. "We do not know of any new king being born."

Before long old King Herod hears of the three Wise Men and their questions and calls together all his learned priests and teachers. He demands that they tell him where this King of the Jews, this Messiah, will be born.

"In Bethlehem of Judea," they tell him, "as hundreds of years ago our great prophet, Micah, told us it would be."

At once Herod sends for the three Wise Men and questions them as to the time the star first appeared. Then the evil and crafty king, secretly wanting to kill the Child, tells them, "Go to Bethlehem. Search for the young Child and when you have found Him bring word to me, so that I may come and worship Him also."

We watch as the three Wise Men come forth from Herod's palace. We know what the Wise Men do not yet know: that they will never come back to this place, for before this night is over an angel will appear, warning them not to return to Herod.

But for now the Wise Men mount their camels, and we follow them as they continue through the city of Jerusalem and onto the winding road to Bethlehem.

"Look up! See, there is the star." It has appeared in the sky more brilliant than ever. The Wise Men rejoice for the star leads them through the gentle hills and fields and into the narrow winding streets of Bethlehem.

Now the star is hovering directly overhead. We have arrived! The Wise Men dismount and go to where the blessed Mother sits, holding the Christ Child. They sink to their knees in worship and present their offerings: a gift of gold, as a symbol of the light of heavenly wisdom that can shine in human thinking; a casket of frankincense for the purest and deepest devotion which can live in human feeling; a jar of myrrh for the good will which human beings, through their deeds, can give to their fellow man and to God.

Like the Wise Men, we too fall to our knees in worship. The Babe, holy and radiant as no other, raises His head and gazes at the three Wise Men and at us. And in His golden glance, love streams forth, touching us all—blessing the whole world.

All creation thrills! The angels sing on high, flowers bloom in winter, animals kneel to adore Him; and we give thanks with all our hearts—for Christ is born; Christ is born!

CHRISTMAS CELEBRATIONS: A SHORT HISTORY

Although the urge to give thanks for the birth of Christ has been in our hearts since the beginning of Christianity, the first Christians did nothing about establishing a firm date for celebrating this wondrous event. The exact birth date of Jesus Christ is not known. The earliest recorded celebrations of His birth took place on January 6, along with Epiphany, which is the festival associated with both the adoration of the three Wise Men and with the baptism of Jesus in the river Jordan.

Later, Christians wanted a special day on which to observe the birth of the Christ Child. The *Feast of the Nativity* began to be celebrated on dates that ranged from November to May. (We are reminded that during this period in history, five different systems for reckoning time were still in use!)

In A.D. 350, the date of December 25 was finally established by a council of the church as the most probable time for the *Feast of the Nativity.* Down through these next 17 centuries this date has become accepted by nearly all Christians around the world.

The history of the celebration of Christmas has never been smooth. Nearly every religion, before Christ, had celebrated some kind of midwinter festival. The Romans celebrated the *Saturnalia* when the return of the sun and the longer hours of daylight promised the coming of spring. The Hebrews celebrated the *Feast of the Dedication of the Temple.* The Druids continued to celebrate the winter solstice; and many Romans remained staunch followers of Mithraism, an ancient religion whose most important feast day, *The Birth of the Unconquered Sun,* took place exactly on December 25.

Nearly every village and town had its own local custom of celebrating one or another of these festivals. It was very natural and understandable that the folk custom of each area would influence and, to some degree, be carried over into the Christian celebration of Christmas.

Many church directives urged Christians to celebrate Christmas after a "heavenly and not an earthly manner." The church gave warnings against overindulging in food and drink, dressing in grotesque costumes and wild animal skins, and against carousing in all forms.

In spite of the high intentions of the church, unchristian practices would crop up from time to time. These practices were so evident at the time of the Protestant Reformation that in Cromwell's England the celebration of Christmas was absolutely forbidden by law. People were even arrested for attending church services on Christmas Day!

Here in America, the Pilgrims brought with them the ban against Christmas festivities, and there was a law against celebrating Christmas in Massachusetts until 1861. Indeed, Christmas did not become a legal holiday in Massachusetts until the middle of the nineteenth century—little more than 100 years ago!

Meanwhile, other settlers from England, Europe, and Scandinavia, including the Dutch, Germans, French, Irish, and people of many other nationalities, came, bringing with them their love of Christmas. They also brought bell ringing, carol singing, candles, the Yule log, Saint Nicholas, and all the customs which have been combined into our modern American celebration of Christmas.

ADVENT HISTORY AND CUSTOMS

The word, 'advent' comes from the Latin word 'adventus,' meaning 'coming' or 'coming in'; and the 'coming in' of Christ has been celebrated since the early years of Christianity. Originally, it was only a time of fasting and prayer before the celebration of Epiphany on January 6. During the fourth century, the date of December 25 was finally set for the *Feast of the Nativity* (the 'Christ Mass'). Then a Christmas Advent became a custom in some places. By the sixth century, Advent had become firmly established as the period beginning four Sundays before Christmas.

During the Middle Ages, Christian social and cultural activities were centered around the church. That is where the great Christmas Eve processions were held, with their shepherds and Wise Men bearing gifts for the Christ Child. These pageants came to be the most important events of the year! There were also Biblical dramas and "mystery plays" performed in the church. Later, the people began to personalize and popularize the wonderful Biblical stories. Soon after, religious drama festivals began to be performed *outside* the church where there were fewer restrictions on the kinds of plays performed.

The *Guild Mystery Plays* became a very important part of the celebration of the Advent season, and some of these plays still survive to this day. The *Carpenter's Guild*, for example, would sponsor a "Story of the Nativity" in which special importance was given to the fact that Joseph was a carpenter.

The *Goldsmiths* produced the mystery play of the Three Magi bringing their golden gifts. The *Fishermen* showed Jesus on the shores of Galilee teaching the disciples to be "Fishers of Men." The *Weavers*, the *Bakers*, and almost all the guilds sponsored Nativity plays based on events of the Bible. Great sums of money were often spent for staging and costumes. As the plays developed, elements of charm and humor, and even of comedy, became more pronounced.

Along with the plays and pageantry, individual family Advent celebrations began. Putting together the Christmas crèche (a miniature Nativity scene) often occupied the entire household for weeks. Sometimes a whole 'Village of Bethlehem' was reproduced, made up of houses and streets and animals as well as the stable with the figures of the Holy Family, shepherds and Wise Men. Only on Christmas Eve was the figure of the Christ Child placed in the manger. All the weeks of creche-building and other activities were to prepare for and welcome the coming of the Babe on the Holy Night—Christmas Eve!

Although storytelling was widely practiced in Germany, Holland, Scandinavia, and England, the actual *origin* of telling stories around the themes of the Advent calendar is not known. We do know, however, that storytelling has always been an important part of family Christmas activities. It is a time for the telling of Bible stories, of stories of inspiration, and of folk tales and legends which lead us to search for an ever-greater understanding of our Creator and the true *Spirit of Christmas.*

MAKE YOUR OWN ADVENT WREATH

It is easy! All it requires are:

- ☆ Some evergreens or holly cut to the desired size.
- ☆ Four low candleholders.
- ☆ Four tall, long-burning candles (red, purple, or white are the most traditional colors).
- ☆ Two or three matching ribbon bows (these are optional).
- ☆ A round frame which can be made from crinkle-textured wire or from smooth wire (both are easily obtainable, usually from florists). Styrofoam circles are also available in a large selection of sizes, from variety stores.

The evergreen (or holly) sprays and candleholders are attached to the round frame to form a circle of green, using string or ribbons to tie them together. If you use the more popular styrofoam, press the greens and candleholders firmly into the material; then use pins or glue to fix the greens and candleholders in position. Place the candles into the holders.

☆   ☆   ☆

On the first Sunday of Advent, or on December 1, light the first candle. Relight the same candle for the first seven days. On the second Sunday (or December 8) relight the first candle and add the light of the second candle. Always relight candles each night which have been lighted before. Repeat for the third candle on the third Sunday (or December 15). On the fourth Sunday (or December 22) you will add the light of the fourth candle (along with the other three) so that all four candles will be burning through Christmas Eve, December 24.

ACKNOWLEDGMENTS

The author extends special thanks and appreciation to authors, publishers, and copyright owners for their courteous permissions to adapt and use selections in *Follow the Star*. Copyright acknowledgments are:

"The Birthday": Four lines from the poem by Phyllis McGinley in *Family Circle*, December, 1964. Used with permission of the publisher. "Heart's Desire": Adapted with permission from *Chi-Wee: The Adventures of a Little Indian Girl* by Grace P. Moon, Copyright © 1925 by Doubleday and Company, Inc. "The Legend of the First Christmas Tree": Adapted with permission from "The Oak Of Geismar" by Henry Van Dyke in *Christmastide*, edited by Wm. J. Roehrenbeck; Copyright © 1948 by Stephen Daye Press, an imprint of Frederick Ungar Publishing Co., Inc. "The Advent Wreath": With permission for the translation use of "Bell Ringing" by Rudolf Steiner. Excerpts from: "The Advent of Our Lord" by Lily M. Gyldenvand from *Christmas: An American Annual of Christmas Literature and Art*, Copyright © 1973, Augsburg Publishing House. Used with permission. "The Little Blind Shepherd": Adapted with permission from "The Little Blind Shepherd," Copyright © 1959 by George Sharp which appeared in *It's Time For Christmas*, edited by Elizabeth Hough Sechrist and Janette Woolsey, published by Macrae Smith Company. "A Candle for Mary": Used with permission of the author, Katherine Keith, Copyright © 1977 and based on stories from the Apocryphal Writings. "The Animal's Christmas": With permission to include selections: "The Gentle Beasts," a Slovakian Carol, translated by Leclair Alger and "The Friendly Beasts," a twelfth-century English poem from *The Christmas Book of Stories and Legends* (edited by Smith & Hazeltine), Copyright © 1944 by Lothrop, Lee & Shepard Co., N.Y. "A Gift for Gramps": Adapted from "A Gift for Gramps" by Aileen Fisher; in *Santa's Footprints* by Walter Retan, et al. Copyright © 1948 by American Book Co., published by E. P. Dutton; and reprinted with their permission. "The Holy Night": Adapted from *Christ Legends* by Selma Lagerlof and translated from the Swedish by Velma Swanston Howard. "Felix": Adapted with permission from "Felix" by Evaleen Stein in *St. Nicholas Magazine*, published by Appleton-Century Company. "The Third Lamb": From *The Third Lamb*, Copyright © 1929 by Anne K. Kyle, adapted with permission by estate of Lydia Rometsch. "A Christmas Gift for the General": Adapted, with permission from "A Christmas Gift for The General" by Jeanette Covert Nolan from *Child Life* Magazine, Copyright © 1937, 1965 by Rand McNally & Company. "Piccola": Adapted with permission from "Piccola" in *My Book House*, edited by Olive Beaupre Miller, Copyright © 1920, 1925, 1928 by The Book House, subsidiary of United Educators, Inc., and from the poem, "Piccola," by Celia Thaxter from *Stories and Poems for Children*, Copyright © 1904 Houghton-Mifflin Company. "How Santa Claus Found the Poorhouse": Adapted with permission from "How Santa Found The Poorhouse," by Sophie Swett, from *Happy Christmas*, edited by Claire H. Bishop, Copyright © 1956 by Stephen Daye Press, imprint of Frederick Ungar Publishing Co., Inc. "Gift from the Earth": Adapted with permission of Tulita Crespi from "Gift of Earth," Copyright © 1934, 1950 by Pachita Crespi from *Christmas, A Book of Stories Old and New*, selected by Alice Dalgliesh, Copyright © 1934, 1950 by Charles Scribner's Sons, Publishers. "The Legend of the Birds": The carol, "Birds" for first and last stanzas Copyright © 1980 Mala Powers; with the other three stanzas translated from an old Czechoslovakian carol. The story, "The Robin," is adapted with permission from *The Golden Book of Christmas Tales*, by James and Lillian Lewicki, Copyright © 1952 by Golden Press, Inc. "Why the Chimes Rang": Adapted with permission from *Why the Chimes Rang*, by Raymond Macdonald Alden, Copyright © 1906, 1935, The Bobbs Merrill Company, Inc. "Don Pedro's Christmas": Adapted with permission from "Don Pedro's Christmas" by Eric P. Kelly in *Child Life* Magazine, Copyright © 1939, 1967 by Rand McNally & Company.

BIBLIOGRAPHY

ALL ABOUT CHRISTMAS, M. R. Krythe, Harper & Brothers, 1954

A WREATH OF CHRISTMAS LEGENDS, Phyllis McGinley, Macmillan Publishing Co., Inc., 1967

AWAY IN A MANGER, Jean Thoburn, Oxford University Press, 1962

THE BOOK OF CHRISTMAS, Reader's Digest Association, 1973

CHRIST LEGENDS, AND OTHER STORIES, Selma Lagerlof, Floris Books, 1977

CHRISTMAS: An American Annual of Christmas Literature and Art, Augsburg Publishing House, annual.

CHRISTMAS, A BOOK OF STORIES OLD AND NEW, Selected by Alice Dalgliesh, Charles Scribner's Sons, 1956

CHRISTMASTIDE, Edited by William J. Roehrenbeck, Librarian, Fordham University, Stephen Daye Press, 1948

CHRISTMAS BOOK OF LEGENDS AND STORIES, Edited by Elva Sophronia Smith & Alice Isabel Hazeltine, Lothrop, Lee & Shepard Company, 1944

THE CHRISTMAS BOOK, Compiled by James Reeves, Dutton, 1968

CHRISTMAS CUSTOMS AROUND THE WORLD, Herbert J. Wernecke, The Westminster Press, 1975

CHRISTMAS CUSTOMS AND TRADITIONS, Clement A. Miles, Dover Publications, Inc., 1976

THE CHRISTMAS LAMB, Sekiya Miyoshi, Dawne-Leigh Publications, 1979

CHRISTMAS STORIES ROUND THE WORLD, Edited by Lois A. Johnson, Rand McNally & Company, 1974

CHRISTMAS EVERYWHERE, Edited by Elizabeth Hough Sechrist, Macrae Smith Company, 1962

46 DAYS OF CHRISTMAS, Dorothy Gladys Spicer, Coward, McCann & Geoghegan, Inc., 1960

THE GOLDEN BOOK OF CHRISTMAS TALES, James and Lillian Lewicki, Golden Press, Inc., 1952

THE GLORY AND PAGEANTRY OF CHRISTMAS, by the editors of Time-Life Books, Hammond, 1974

HIGHLIGHTS FOR CHILDREN, Selected Christmas stories from the November/December Magazine issues through 1979

HOLLY, REINDEER, AND COLORED LIGHTS, Edna Barth, The Seabury Press, 1971

THE ILLUSTRATED BOOK OF CHRISTMAS FOLKLORE, Tristan Potter Coffin, The Seabury Press, 1973

IT'S TIME FOR CHRISTMAS, Edited by Elizabeth Hough Sechrist and Janette Woolsey, Macrae Smith Co., 1959

JOY TO THE WORLD, Ruth Sawyer, Little Brown, 1966

MERRY CHRISTMAS TO YOU, Compiled by Wilhelmina Harper, Dutton, 1965

MY BOOK HOUSE, in 12 volumes, Edited by Olive Beaupre Miller, Selected Christmas Stories, Legends and Poems, The Book House For Children, 1971

NATIVITY STORIES, Alan Howard, Dawne-Leigh Publications, 1980

PARENT'S MAGAZINE'S CHRISTMAS HOLIDAY BOOK, Parent's Magazine Press, 1972

SAINT NICHOLAS, LIFE AND LEGENDS, Martin Ebon, Harper & Row, Publishers, 1975

TAKE JOY, Tasha Tudor, The World Publishing Company, 1966

THIS WAY TO CHRISTMAS, Ruth Sawyer, Harper and Brothers, 1944

TOLD UNDER THE CHRISTMAS TREE, Selections by the Literature Committee of The Association for Childhood Education, The Macmillan Co., 1949

WHY THE CHIMES RANG, Raymond Macdonald Alden, The Bobbs Merrill Company, 1935